JASON

River Valley Lawmen Series
Book Two

CHERYL WRIGHT

Contents:

JASON

RIVER VALLEY LAWMEN SERIES

Book Two

Copyright ©2018 by Cheryl Wright

Cover Artist: <u>Black Widow Books</u>

Thanks

Thanks to my very dear friends (and authors), Margaret Tanner and Susan Horsnell for their enduring encouragement and friendship.

Thanks also to Alan, my husband of over 45 years, who has been a relentless supporter of my writing for many years.

And last, but by no means least, thank you to all my wonderful readers who encourage me to continue writing these stories. It is such a joy to me knowing so many of you enjoy reading my stories. I love writing them as much as you love reading them.

Chapter One

With lights and sirens going full blast, Officer Jason Sawyer sped to the location he was given.

The fire department were already there when he arrived. Not that they could do much except be there for support and keep any onlookers at bay.

He almost ran up the two hundred and fifty-four steps from the foyer to the roof-top.

He took off his police issue hat and unlatched the gun holster sitting on his hip. Not that he thought he'd need it.

Young Daniel Jenkins wasn't a danger to anyone but himself, so the gun was probably overkill. The officer winced. Protocol. He hated it sometimes.

The teenager had his back turned as Officer Sawyer approached, but suddenly he spun around to face him.

"Get back!" Daniel shouted at him, tears running down his face, and Jason threw his hands in the air.

"Daniel," he said gently. "I'm not here to hurt you. Or arrest you." He took two measured steps forward, and Daniel took three steps back.

"Don't." The teenager looked more scared than before. "I'm, I'm going to jump," he said. "My life is over." The boy stared down at his feet. "No one wants me here. No one will miss me, not even my family."

Jason felt for the boy. Life was so much harder for teenagers these days. Especially in a small town like River Valley where everyone knew everything about you.

"It's not true," he told the boy. "Your family loves you. You have friends, lots of friends."

The boy's eyes spoke of the rage he felt. "None of that is true," he spat out, then suddenly stood at the edge of the barrier and looked to the ground. "Everyone hates me," he added, as he continued to stare below them.

"Daniel, your mother is on her way here now."

The boy nodded and continued to stare at the scene playing out in the street below.

Jason's heartbeat quickened as the boy stepped up onto the safety barrier. He watched helplessly as Daniel swayed. "Don't do it, Daniel," he said softly, and walked toward the edge, but away from the boy.

This kid was breaking his heart. What could be so bad you wanted to end your young life?

He looked down. A small crowd had gathered, and he watched as a woman got out of a police car. "Is that your mom?" he asked gently.

The boy was silent but nodded.

Jason took a deep breath. "Think about what you're doing Daniel," he said softly, and with compassion. "Do you want your mom to remember you as a splot on the sidewalk?"

The youth shook his head and his face crumpled.

Jason moved quickly toward the boy, but without startling him, and wrapped his arm around Daniel's waist.

He pulled him off the ledge and into a big bear hug before he could change his mind.

As they walked toward the exit, they heard applause from below. He could only imagine the relief Daniel's mother was feeling right now.

~~~

Heavily pregnant, Melanie Bishop struggled down the steps of the bus.

As the driver pulled her scant luggage from the storage compartment, she wondered what she would do next.

Now that she'd arrived in River Valley, she needed to rethink her situation.
~~~

Did she really want to confront her baby's father? Would he even remember her?

She was emotional, whether from baby hormones or her current situation she wasn't sure. One thing she did know; she was totally exhausted. She'd spent the last three days on that dusty and dirty bus, and longed for a proper bed to sleep in. Whether or not it would happen, was a totally different story.

Whatever was ahead of her, she needed to rest. She could barely keep her eyes open. She slumped on the seat at the bus stop and leaned back.

It would only be for a moment or two she told herself.

"Ma'am?" She awoke with a fright. At first she didn't know where she was. Glancing around, it all came back to her. *How long had she been sleeping?* "Ma'am," the man said again, as he leaned closer.

"Are you all right, Ma'am?" The police officer asked, tipping his hat as he straightened up.

She let out a huge sigh, and her eyes fluttered as she tried to get used to the light.

"I'm fine," she said. "Just really tired from a long bus trip." She smiled, but he didn't return the smile.

"Officer Josh Wrangler, Ma'am," he said, introducing himself.

She put her hand above her eyes to block the afternoon sun. "I'm Melanie Bishop. I'm in River Valley, right?" She could easily have gotten off at the wrong place. She'd been so disoriented when she'd awoken as the bus arrived.

"Yes, Ma'am. You sure are," he said, looking at her curiously. "Can I take you somewhere, Ma'am." Concern was written all over his face.

Take her somewhere? Sure. Where that somewhere was, she had no idea at this stage. She straightened up on the seat and began to stand.

Her head was spinning, and she felt herself go sideways. No! She couldn't risk hurting her baby. She felt tears trickling down her face.

Two strong hands held her but as he sat her back down again her waters broke. She let out a squeal.

She stared into his face. He looked to the ground, and calmly continued to seat her.

She heard him talking into his communications device, then everything went quiet.

"It's okay," she heard him say. "The paramedics are coming. Don't panic."

She sniffed. This is not how it was supposed to be. "I came to see my baby's father," she said. "This wasn't supposed to happen." She sniffed again. "It's too early."

She looked up into his face with tears streaming down her face. His was still blank. But she knew that was what cops were trained to do.

"Ma'am, Ms. Bishop," he said. "If you don't mind me asking, who *is* the baby's father? I can try and locate him for you."

She closed her eyes momentarily then then looked him squarely in the face. "Officer Jason Sawyer," she said, then watched as Officer Wrangler stumbled backwards.

<p style="text-align:center">~~~</p>

Jason arrived at the hospital emergency department, flanked by fellow officer and friend, Lucas Drury.

He was too stunned to drive to the hospital alone.

Josh Wrangler met him in the waiting area and escorted the pair to the woman in question.

She lay sleeping on a hospital bed.

"Melanie?" he said, the moment he lay eyes on her. She didn't move. He leaned forward and kissed her cheek.

Josh stepped forward. "She said her name is Melanie Bishop, and you're the baby's father," he offered.

Jason's heart began to beat quickly. Baby? Father? Him?

Couldn't be.

Or could it?

He counted the months back on his fingers and stopped in his tracks.

The timeline was right. He'd woken up one day to discover she'd left town.

And not a word from Melanie. Not even a note.

She'd broken his heart, shattered it into little pieces. He'd had feelings for her, strong feelings.

He'd resented her at the time for leaving him like that, and those feelings came flooding back as he looked down into her sleeping face.

He looked at her swollen belly. He reached out and gently placed his hand there. Inside that belly was his baby.

His baby!

His head was spinning at the sudden revelation. An hour ago, he was arresting a man for drunk and disorderly.

Now he was standing next to the love of his life, learning for the first time he was about to become a father.

This wasn't the way he expected his day to turn out.

The curtains were suddenly thrown back and a woman strolled in. "I'm Molly," she said. "Dr Molly, and I will be delivering this baby.

Jason's head shot up. "Now? As in right now?" He'd just found out he was going to be a father, and now he finds out it's immediate.

Molly glanced at him in sympathy. "Her waters broke," she said. "We can't delay, or infection could set in."

Jason nodded his understanding.

"Are you the baby's father? Come with me," she said, not waiting for an answer, and Jason followed, his head still in a spin.

Twenty minutes ago, he was at the sheriff's office filling out paperwork for the arrest. Blissfully single. And now he was about to get an instant family. *This couldn't be happening!*

But it was. And he needed to cop in on the chin and do whatever needed to be done.

Melanie, now awake, was wheeled out of the emergency department and taken to the birthing suite. Jason gingerly followed.

"One more push and your baby will be delivered," Molly said.

The last couple of hours had been hell. Not only for Melanie who was giving birth, but for Jason. *How the hell did this happen?*

Okay, so he knew *how* it happened, but why didn't he know about it before? Why didn't Melanie tell him?

Then it hit him. He'd openly declared his *confirmed bachelor* status. Always.

Even when he and Melanie were going out.

It was more a joke than anything, to try and stop Aunt Lizzie from hooking him up with someone he wasn't interested in.

She wasn't his aunt, but everyone called her aunt, even the sheriff. She owned Aunt Lizzie's Kitchen and was notorious for her match-making. Sometimes the sheriff even helped her.

He'd decided he wasn't going to get caught in her snare.

No way. He wasn't going there, so made the fact known that he was never leaving bachelorhood.

So now he knew why she'd left.

It was his fault. Totally his fault. He'd repeatedly told everyone he was a confirmed bachelor and didn't want to be tied down.

Now he fully understood. Once Melanie realized she was pregnant, she must have taken off, not wanting to tell him.

Hell. This was all his fault. He should have been there for her all these months. Not find out like this. He had no idea what she'd endured in the interim.

"Hold her hand, dad." Dr Molly brought him out of his wayward thoughts.

His head shot up and he looked at Melanie who was obviously in need of his support. He grabbed her hand and she held tight.

"And push!"

The baby arrived in one big swoosh.

Jason looked at Melanie, then his baby, and fainted.

~~~

Melanie was sitting up in the hospital bed looking decidedly better than she had when she'd arrived, despite it being only a few hours since she'd given birth.

Next to her in a hospital basinet was her baby.
~~~

Their baby. When would he wrap his head around that fact?

A little girl. They had a daughter, and her name was Lily.

Lily Rose. Totally Melanie's choice. Jason wasn't sure how he felt about that but loved the name she'd chosen.

He stood in the doorway and watched them quietly, then stepped into the room, and Melanie's head shot up.

Her face was blank. Did she think he was mad at her?

He sure as hell should be. But he wasn't. More than anything he was confused.

Why would she do this to him?

He stepped forward and handed her a huge bunch of flowers. She smiled, and just like he remembered, her smile lit up the room.

She glanced across to the baby, and her face softened. "Come and see your daughter," she told him quietly. "Isn't she beautiful?"

He moved the few steps to the basinet and stared into it. His chest tightened. She really was his baby daughter, not that he had any doubt. "Yes, she is," he said, swallowing down the emotion that threatened to overtake him.

He touched his finger to her cheek. "She's so soft," he said, not sure what else to say. He knew so little about babies.

A nurse fluttered into the room. "How are you doing, Melanie? You must tell me if you have any pain," she said, glancing across to Jason. "You must be dad. Otherwise you aren't allowed in here."

"This is Jason," Melanie quickly said. "Lily's father."

Lily's father.

It sounded good, and yet it sounded totally alien to him. How long would it take to get used to hearing that?

Most men had at least six months to get used to the thought, but he'd had less than a day. What a shock to the system that was!

The baby began to cry. Jason observed her in the basinet but stood where he was. Cemented to the ground. Not sure what he should do.

The nurse turned to him. "Pick her up," she said.

He stared at her in horror. She let out a visible sigh.

"Sit," she said, slightly irritated.

He did as he was told. Before he knew what was happening, Lily had been placed in his arms. "I, I don't know anything about babies," he said, feeling suddenly scared.

The nurse glared at him, hands on hips. "Guess what, fella? You're about to learn." She went back to tending to Melanie.

"Put her to your shoulder and pat her back gently," the nurse offered, a little more genially. "Mum is going to feed her in a minute. But I need to sort *her* out first."

Jason swallowed. *What if she wriggled in his arms and he dropped her?*

He held her away from himself and decided this tiny creature couldn't wriggle. She was wrapped way too tight for that.

He let out a sigh of relief.

Strangely enough he began to feel comfortable with the little angel in his arms. He lay her in the cradle of his arms and stared down into her face.

He took a deep breath and inhaled her fragrance. She smelled like... baby.

She was his baby. His daughter. It was so hard to take in.

She had dark hair like his, and lots of it. Her nose was a little button just like Melanie's, but she had his eyes. It was like staring into a mirror, looking at those pretty blue eyes.

"I'll take her now," the nurse said gently. Perhaps she'd understood his quiet contemplation? *Maybe all new dads are like this?* He had no idea, but it had certainly been a shock to the system.

She passed Lily over to her mother, who was ready to breast-feed her baby. Jason turned his head.

"Silly," Melanie told him, laughing. "You've seen way more of me than this."

"I guess," he said, embarrassed. The nurse looked at him strangely, and he felt the heat move up his neck to his face.

As the nurse instructed Melanie how to feed, Jason stood. "Where are you going?"

Melanie looked concerned. Did she think he was going to run out on her? He certainly hoped not.

"I need coffee."

The nurse scowled at him. "Sit. Stay here with your wife. She needs your support right now." Her expression softened. "Coffee can wait. Spend some time with your family." She smiled, which was new. Mostly she just appeared to be mad at him.

"Please, Jason," Melanie asked softly as she fed Lily. And he felt like a heel for ever wanting to leave.

"Dad," the nurse said.

"Jason." Would he ever get used to being called dad?

"Your baby needs supplies. Clothes, diapers, socks, singlets and more." She looked to Melanie. "You don't have any here, right? I couldn't find any while you slept."

"No," she said sadly. "I don't." She closed her eyes, as though blocking out the hurt.

"It's not a problem," Jason said, and Melanie's eyes flew open as heat slowly moved up her face.

He reached across and touched her on the arm. "It's fine," he said. "I'll make sure she's properly fitted out."

The nurse laughed at his words. He wasn't sure what was so funny.

He kissed Melanie on the forehead then headed for the door. "Don't come back for a couple of hours," the nurse said sternly. "Melanie needs to rest. Giving birth is a major ordeal."

He nodded then left, wondering just what he had ahead of him.

~~~

Sheriff Chase Callahan listened intently as Jason told him the situation.

"And until a few hours ago, I had no idea of any of this," he said, his arms flailing. "I think I'm still in shock. One minute I'm on patrol, and suddenly I'm a father."

He sat back in his seat and waited for his superior to speak.

He said nothing.

"I, I, er, don't know what I'm supposed to do now," Jason said, breaking the silence.

Chase leaned forward, closer to Officer Sawyer. "What you do now, Jason, is whatever needs to be done." His face seemed set in stone, and although Jason knew him to be a reasonable man, he wasn't sure how all this sat with Chase. Being such short notice and all.

He looked at his watch. "You've probably got time to catch the shops and get enough baby supplies to get you through the next day or two. I'll see if my sister-in-law can help you out tomorrow. My niece is
~~~

only a few months old, so she will be able to advise what you'll need."

Jason nodded, but his head was so full of information, he was beginning to feel confused.

"I can give you a few weeks off, if that helps," Chase said. "Actually, let's make it a month. You've got a ton of leave owing."

Jason wasn't sure about this turn of events. "I don't think…"

"Sleep on it but given the situation you'll probably need a bit of time off. Let's get together again sometime in the next couple of days and decide where to go from here," he said. "But Jason," he looked the other man in the eye. "Don't stress about your job. You're too good an officer to lose."

He stood and extended his hand, and Jason felt relief. "Thank you, Sheriff," he said. "I truly appreciate it."

He left the sheriff's office with a whole new agenda on his mind.

~~~

"Singlets, dresses, and leggings," he counted them off on his fingers. "There was something else?"

The sales assistant approached. "Can I help you, sir," she said, taking in the clothing in his basket.

He sighed with relief. "New baby," he said. "I know I've forgotten something, but I can't remember what."
~~~

The assistant grinned and took the clothing, going through it as she folded. "You seem to have everything except socks, matinee jackets, and diapers," she said. "Or perhaps you have those already?"

She walked toward the front counter and deposited his purchases.

"No, nothing," he said. "This was all kinda last minute. I didn't..." he let his words trail off. River Valley was a small town, and he didn't want gossip spreading about his personal business.

"I definitely need diapers, and socks too," he said. "And whatever else you think I need. The smallest you've got?"

She rang up his purchases and frowned at him. "These won't last long," she said. "Only a couple of days."

He sighed with the knowledge. "I know," he said shrugging. "Baby came early. We were unprepared." Well, it was the truth. Wasn't it? "I'll be back in a day or two, hopefully with a friend. She knows more about this stuff than I do," he said, paying for his purchases and hoping Missy Callahan was available to help him out.

Jason left the store, anticipating seeing his daughter again soon, but knowing he had to wait until after dinner.

~~~

The little bell on the door tinkled, and Aunt Lizzie came rushing out from the kitchen.
~~~

"Jason!" she said excitedly. "Congratulations!" She ran around to his side of the counter and hugged him.

So much for keeping the news secret.

"I am so happy for you. And Melanie of course." She pulled back and smiled. "I always knew you two were meant for each other. This is amazing news."

Jason stared down at her. The grapevine sure worked fast in this town. "Thanks," he said, still rather shell-shocked.

"Okay, give," Lizzie said. "What is the baby's name, and how heavy was she?" Obviously, the grapevine wasn't as efficient as he'd first thought.

"Lily Rose," he said, then frowned. "I don't know how heavy. Does it matter?" he asked, puzzled why anyone needed that information.

Lizzie waved her hands in front of her. "Lily Rose is a beautiful name. How is Melanie?"

"Melanie is doing well," he said. "For someone who has just had a baby." Not just any baby. His baby. His baby he had no idea about until earlier today.

He was trying not to let it get to him, but it did. Why didn't she tell him? A phone call would have done the job, but nothing. Silence for six whole months, and then he's presented with a baby.

His baby. Lily Rose. The light of his life.

Lizzie hugged him again. "It will all turn out all right," she said, then moved behind the counter. "What can I get for you, young fella?"

"I need some dinner," he told her. "Then it's back to the hospital."

"You leave it to me," she said, then disappeared into the kitchen.

Five minutes later Charlotte Dolan, Aunt Lizzie's Kitchen chef, brought out a roast chicken dinner. "It smells amazing," he told her, and wondered how many times over the next weeks he'd be having dinner here. "Thank you."

"You're welcome. Anything else I can get for you, Officer Sawyer," she said.

"Jason," he said. "Please call me Jason. And I desperately need coffee." Jason worked with Charlotte's husband, Deputy Chris Dolan. He thought by now she'd feel comfortable calling him by his first name.

Charlotte laughed. "What is it with cops and coffee? Extra large coffee on its way."

But Lizzie was two steps ahead of them both, and had already prepared it, and put the mug of the steaming beverage in front of him. "Enjoy, young fella," she said, then left him alone with his thoughts.

He knew that after everything that had happened today, coffee would really hit the spot.

"They're beautiful, Jason," Melanie said, going through the pile of baby clothes."

She still looked tired.

Not that he was surprised. After that long grueling bus trip, and then giving birth not long after arriving in River Valley, that's got to knock it out of you.

"I need to get more," he said quickly. "But this will get you through the next couple of days."

She nodded.

"The sheriff is going to ask Missy to help me." She looked up suddenly and he realized she didn't know the news. "Rory and Missy have a baby now. Little Chloe is a few months old, so Missy is an old hand."

He walked over to the basinet and his sleeping daughter. "She's beautiful, Melanie," he said in a whisper. "But I really wish..."

Just then the same nurse entered. Great timing. Not.

"Ah, baby clothes. Thanks dad," she said, taking the clothes from Melanie. Now we can dress your little doll up."

She proceeded to fill the cupboard drawers with baby clothes, withholding some to use immediately.

"I'll get more tomorrow," he offered.

The nurse nodded. She began to wheel the baby out of the room. Jason frowned.

"Don't worry, I'm just going to change her diaper and her clothes," she said. "I'll bring her back shortly."

"Melanie," he said as soon as the nurse disappeared out of the room. "We need to talk."

She looked at him, terror written across her face. Then glanced down into her lap, where her hands were entwined. "I'm sorry," she said. "I never intended to dump all this on you."

"Dump?" he said. "My baby is not a pile of rubbish to be dumped!" Now he was feeling angry.

She looked hurt. "That's not what I meant, I hope you understand that." She reached out and covered his hand with hers. "I'm really tired, Jason," she said. "I can't even think straight at the moment."

He nodded his understanding. "Maybe we should wait until tomorrow to talk, when I can think straight."

He hoped by then he'd have his head wrapped around all this too.

<div align="center">~~~</div>

It was a new day, with a whole new perspective.

He arrived at the hospital a little after ten. In time to see Melanie feeding their baby. It certainly was a sight to cherish.

He stood in the doorway and watched quietly. "Morning," he said softly, not wanting to startle Lily.

Melanie smiled, and the baby continued to suckle. "Good morning," she said, still smiling.

She looked much better today. There were still circles under her eyes, but no where near as bad as they were yesterday. She'd endured a lot, and he really hadn't appreciated that.

But then he'd had a lot to take in.

After all, it's not every day you become an instant dad. He just wished she'd told him earlier.

He sighed, then moved around to sit next to the hospital bed. "She looks sweet in her new clothes," Jason said quietly. Suddenly Lily began to cry, and he felt distressed. "What's wrong with her? Should I call the nurse?" he asked, panicked.

Melanie laughed. "I took her off the breast, that's all. She's got wind."

A nurse strolled into the room. "I need to check Melanie's stomach," she said, looking directly at Jason.

"You take the baby and burp her while I do. Thanks." She passed Lily over to her father.

He wasn't sure what to do and said so. "Sorry, you're a *new* dad," she said. "I should have known – you are smitten."

With the baby placed on his shoulder, Jason began to gently pat her little back until she brought up wind. Then she started crying again. He stood and walked around with her until she fell asleep.

He surprised even himself, then lay his precious baby in her basinet.

By now the nurse had left the room to get Melanie a well-deserved cup of tea.

"We need to talk," Jason said softly, not wanting to disturb the baby.

Melanie took a deep breath. "Okay." She sounded wary, as though not sure what to expect. "If you don't want her, I..."

"What the hell, Melanie!" Jason was horrified. *Why would he not want his precious daughter? Why would she even think that?* "Of course I want her. What are you thinking?"

She put her hands in her lap and looked down at them. "Look at me, Melanie," he said. "I will take care of both of you." She lifted her face and stared into his eyes. "Just tell me why you took off like that." As much as he tried not to be, he still felt hostility toward her.

She should have told him sooner. He could have been there for her.

She braced her back and her lips went into a tight line. "You didn't want a baby. You said you were a confirmed bachelor," she said, her voice breaking. Her voice went suddenly quiet. "You didn't even love me." Tears welled up in her eyes. "I certainly wasn't going to force you into fatherhood."

He sat in silence. *That was then.* Before.

Before he met Melanie.

Before he fell in love with her.

His heart had broken when she left without a word. He had no idea what he'd done to push her away. He'd thought about searching for her, but if she didn't want to be found...

He swallowed down the huge lump in his throat. "Melanie, I..." What did he say? It was too late. She'd been gone six months. He'd been so in love with her, and foolishly, had never said the words.

His thoughts were all over the place now. *Did he still love her? He couldn't say.* He was in a constant state of confusion since he found out yesterday.

He was certainly annoyed at being excluded from the past six months. Of being there for Melanie and Lily. Ensuring the baby was okay, and that Melanie was well cared for.

A thought suddenly struck him. "Where have you been the past six months?" She had little in the way of family, so it was doubtful she'd have stayed with them.

A tear trickled down her face. "In women's shelters mostly."

"Damn it, Melanie!" He shoved the chair back and paced the room. Lily began to cry. He looked down into the basinet, admonishing himself for startling his daughter.

He leaned down and gently picked her up, placing her on his shoulder. "Shhhhh," he whispered, trying to settle the baby down again.

"She's probably wet," Melanie told him. "Bring her here and I'll change her diaper." She put out her arms, but Jason was reluctant to let go. "Please," she said, almost pleading.

He handed the baby over and took a diaper from the drawer.

"What are we going to do?" He wasn't sure he could get past this. Anything could have happened to Melanie out there alone. Or to his baby. He cringed at the thought.

He was still pacing the room. He was beyond annoyed and couldn't stay still. "Look," he said, placing the freshly changed baby back in her bed. "I have to go. There's so much to do. Including buying more clothes."

She nodded but said nothing. Fresh tears stained her cheeks.

He sat down again, then took her hand. "Melanie, I'm not sure we can ever move forward from this." It was true. He wasn't sure he could forgive her.

Or himself for not saying how he felt. This was just as much his fault. And now he'd regret it for the rest of his life.

She yanked her hand away and swiped at her cheeks. "I'm sorry," she said quietly.

He nodded, then left without a word.

~~~

Missy promised to meet him outside the infant supply store. To his surprise, Rory was there instead.

"Congratulations, Dad," Rory said as he hugged Jason. "It's a wonderful feeling, isn't it?"

Jason looked at the ground. "I guess," he said honestly.

Rory stared at him. "What the hell, bro?" He looked annoyed.

"Where's Missy? I need to get these baby things."

Rory continued to stare. Only now it became a glare. "She's inside with Chloe, browsing. Listen Jason, let's walk for a bit." They walked toward a local park. "I know fatherhood is not easy. And I know how it all panned out." As they arrived at their destination, he indicated for Jason to sit down next to him.

"I love that little girl," Jason said, looking at his boots.

Rory slapped him on the back. "Great! So what's the problem?"

"She betrayed me," he said, staring at Rory. "I mean," he swallowed hard. "She left me when she found out she was pregnant. Didn't give me any choices."
~~~

Jason was a tough cop, but right now he wanted to cry. His emotions were starting to get the better of him. He braced his shoulders and fisted his hands. He was not going to let Rory see how upset he was, but the other man was watching his every move.

"Jason," Rory said gently. "We've been friends for many years; went to school together, even threw stones at the abandoned homestead together."

That made Jason smile. "Yeah, we did," he said, even managing a laugh. "Got our asses kicked too when the sheriff found out."

"My point is," Rory continued. "You can tell me anything. Ask me anything. I want to help you," he finished.

Jason sat where he was, not saying a word. He wasn't sure what to say if he was honest with himself.

"Man, I can't help you if you won't help yourself." Rory let out an audible sigh. "What are your plans?"

"Plans? What do you mean?" Jason was confused.

"Melanie just arrived back in town, right?" When Jason nodded, he continued. "Where is she going to stay? Are you taking her and the baby back to your place?"

He hadn't thought that far ahead. "My place? Um..."

"Do you, or do you not want to be a family? To see your baby every day? To see her grow up?"

His head shot up. Of course he wanted to see Lily every day, and watch her grow into a beautiful young girl, but he wasn't sure if that was an option.

Would Melanie even agree to it?

"Yes," he said quietly. His voice slightly above a whisper. "But I'm not sure it's what Melanie wants."

Rory nodded. "Right now, think about the immediate future. They have nowhere to stay. You have a big cabin, with plenty of space."

Everything Rory said made sense. He was on the outside looking in, which is exactly what Jason needed at the moment – he was not in the right frame of mind. But he still had reservations. "What if she doesn't agree?"

Rory slapped him on the back. "Let's worry about that later."

They stood and headed back to the store where Missy had a pile of clothes sitting on Chloe's buggy. Rory strolled over to her and hugged her tight. Jason watched as he kissed her on the cheek.

Their love for each other was palpable.

He wanted that with Melanie but wasn't sure it would ever happen. Could ever happen.

"Hey Jason. Congratulations," Missy said.

"Yeah, thanks," he said quietly. She looked at Rory, apparently picking up on Jason's desolation.

"He needs everything," Rory said, matter-of-factly.

"Everything?" Missy asked. "I hope your wallet is full," she said.

"Money is the least of my worries," Jason said. "Just tell me what I need, because I have no idea."

Rory grabbed a shopping trolley and they began their big adventure in the baby superstore. Jason was convinced he'd seen the sales assistant rubbing her hands together as they gathered up a basinet and all the bedding that went with it, a buggy, baby clothes, a change mat, and what seemed like a year's supply of diapers.

"Oh, and a baby bath," Missy said. "Can't forget that. Do you have soft towels? Babies need soft towels, not hard ones like I know you cowboys use." She laughed, and Rory's face lit up. She reached over and grabbed some towels, baby wash, and baby powder.

Rory carefully chose a baby carrier for Jason's vehicle.

Babies sure needed a lot of stuff.

Strangely enough he'd enjoyed buying for his little girl and wondered how long he'd be able to do that.

Chapter Three

Nearly a week later, Melanie and Lily were finally allowed to leave the hospital.

It was wonderful and terrifying all at the same time. He'd spent many hours preparing his home to accommodate the pair; setting up the basinet with the bedding, making sure it was sufficient for little Lily.

He'd also moved a chest of drawers into that room, filled with diapers and baby clothes, as well as the baby bath and bathing accessories.

Melanie's room would be next to Lily's, so she could hear her easily, and tend to her needs.

As he walked them out of the hospital, Jason wasn't sure what to expect. He still had time off work, as the sheriff had generously allowed him to spend time with his new family. Luckily he had plenty of leave available.

He left Melanie sitting in the hospital waiting area while he got his truck. Rory had helped him fit the baby carrier to ensure it was done correctly.

Lily was sleeping peacefully when he'd left them, but wondered if she would be disturbed when he strapped her in. He hoped not.

Melanie was standing in the pick-up area when he arrived. "I told you to wait inside," he said, slightly annoyed. He didn't want Lily to get a chill.

"It's a beautiful day," she said. "The fresh air will do Lily and me good."

He knew she was right. They'd been stuck inside for days. She passed the baby over and Jason strapped her in, careful to ensure he did it correctly and she was safe.

He placed Melanie's bag with both her clothes and the baby's in the back.

"All set," he asked when she was finally settled in.

She nodded, and they were on their way.

It was about half an hour from the hospital to his house, and neither of them said a word. Lily slept the whole way. She had already proved to be a good baby, mostly only waking to be changed or fed.

Jason hoped she stayed that way. Once he was back at work, he'd be back on shifts, and often needed to sleep through the day.

She began to cry as they turned into his driveway.

Melanie looked at her watch. "It's a little early for her feed, so she's probably wet."

"Smells like a messy diaper to me," he said, winding down his window to let in some fresh air." He wasn't sure he'd get used to this but was grateful for his beautiful daughter.

Melanie sniffed the air. "You could be right," she said, then sighed.

Jason jumped out as soon as they pulled up and unlocked the cabin door.

"You're in the spare room, and I've put Lily in the other room," he said when he got back outside. "I moved the single bed out of there to make more room."

Melanie frowned at him. "You know this is only temporary, right?"

"Yeah, sure," he said, hoping that somehow it could become permanent. He took the bag from the vehicle and followed Melanie inside.

"Oh my goodness, Jason," she said, almost in tears when she saw everything he'd bought. "You didn't have to..."

He interrupted. "Yes, I did. She's my daughter, and she needed stuff." He knew he sounded gruff, but he didn't need her second-guessing him. Lily was his baby, and that's all there was to it.

He took the bag into the spare room for Melanie. "When you're up to it, we'll go to town and get clothes for you."

Melanie protested, but he was having none of it. "You need supplies, and that's all there is about it." Why did she have to fight him all the time?

"Thank you," she mouthed, then turned to change Lily's dirty bottom.

~~~

Jason stumbled out of bed the next morning.

Having a baby in the house was not conducive to good sleep. But this was his daughter he was talking about.

The more he thought about it, the more he realized he had the easy end of the bargain. Melanie would have been awake a lot of the night. At least he got to sleep through.

He moved toward the kitchen to put the jug on. He needed coffee!

As if right on cue, Lily began to cry. And cry. And cry.

Where was Melanie?

He crept down the passageway to find she was sound asleep. He stood in the doorway and watched her sleeping. He really missed doing that.

They were together close to a year, and to Jason's mind, they were close. Close enough that he was going to ask her to marry him.

And then she disappeared without warning.
~~~

He shook his head trying to shake away the memories. The hurt feelings came tumbling back like an avalanche down a hillside.

And his heart ached.

Lily was still crying, and Melanie was still sleeping, so he went to Lily's room and picked the baby up. She stopped crying almost immediately.

She was wet through. He fumbled for a moment or two, not sure what to do next, then remembered what he'd been taught at the hospital – get all the clothes, diapers etc out before removing the baby from the basinet.

He put her back and the crying started up again. He sighed.

At least he knew where everything was, since he'd put them there.

After getting everything organized, he lifted Lily out again and lay her on the changing mat. Even her blanket was wet.

Jason began to peel off her tiny clothes and looked his baby over. He gently touched her soft cheek with his finger. Her little hands went up to her face, and her tiny fingers grabbed hold of his and his heart fluttered.

He made this little girl.

Staring down into her tiny face, he again saw himself in her eyes. They were cobalt blue and almond shaped like his.

Checking her over further, he discovered the baby was drenched, almost from head to toe. At that point he decided to put her back into the basinet again and bath her.

That could be quite an experience. Especially since it would be his first time alone.

Jason was rather taken aback with the task ahead of him, but he had no intentions of waking Melanie. She needed the sleep.

He made sure the water was only tepid, testing it with his elbow as he'd been shown by the midwife.

Once again, he lifted the baby out of the basinet and placed her on the changing mat. This time he completely undressed her and gently placed her in the baby bath.

She lay back against his arm, her little legs splashing in the water. He used the washer to clean her, then let her play for a few minutes. She was content there, and he didn't want to break the spell.

He stared down at her, and still found it hard to believe he was a dad. A father. This baby's father.

It was going to take a while to let it all sink in.

He pulled her out as the water was beginning to cool down and placed her on a towel. He wrapped her up and gently dried her tiny body, adding a diaper as soon as he could. He didn't want another mess to clean up.

He smiled to himself. *Would he really care?* It was a moot question because he knew he wouldn't.

Lily was quickly dressed, and he wrapped her in a clean blanket as best he could, then placed her on his shoulder and patted her back.

He hoped to give her mother a little more sleeping time.

"Good morning." The words startled him.

He turned to see Melanie in her robe, sleep tousled hair. It brought back so many memories – of the good times they'd spent together.

He'd loved this woman so much. *Why the hell didn't he tell her?*

He swallowed down his regrets and focused on the baby again. "Good morning," he said. "She's probably hungry," he added as he gazed into Lily's face.

Melanie looked around the room. "You've been busy." She put out her arms for their little bundle, and Jason reluctantly handed her over. He knew it had to happen. She needed to be fed.

But he felt bereft without her in his arms.

What would he do when Melanie left again?

~~~

He made coffee while Melanie fed the baby.

He'd had no idea having a baby in the house would change his life entirely. They'd never discussed having children. He wasn't sure it was something Melanie wanted.

Hell, he hadn't discussed anything with her. Anything that mattered, anyway.
~~~

His biggest regret was not telling her how he felt. What a fool he was. If he'd done that, things would be different.

Wouldn't they?

Instead of treating each other like strangers, they'd be rejoicing the birth of their baby. Instead of hedging around each other, they'd be embracing.

Instead of taking turns looking after the baby, they'd be working together.

He was such a fool. Things could have been so different between them.

As he poured coffee for Melanie, he pondered Rory's words. He'd asked if Jason wanted a family. If he wanted to see Lily everyday. If he wanted to see her grow up.

He did. Of course he did. But would Melanie let him? That was the million-dollar question.

He wondered if it was as simple as Rory made out. He was not married to Melanie.

They were not madly in love. Although there was a time he felt that way. Maybe he still did? He was still in a state of confusion, and honestly didn't know what he thought right now.

All was not right in his world. In fact it was downright terrible.

He stared down into the coffee mug. He'd been stirring Melanie's coffee for the past two minutes at least. His thoughts were getting away with him, and he was unable to function properly.

He carried the hot beverage into the loungeroom where Melanie was feeding Lily. "She seems a bit happier now," he ventured, placing the mug on the side table.

Melanie nodded, then started to put the baby to her shoulder. "I can do that if you like," he said, wanting to hold the baby again.

"Sure, why not?" she said. "Besides, I really need coffee."

He walked about the house as he patted Lily's back gently. She was such a sweet little thing, and he was surely going to miss her when her mother left.

He swallowed down his distress. He didn't want to lose either of them, but he wasn't sure he could forgive Melanie for up and leaving him like that.

It wasn't as though there was a problem. They were getting on like a house on fire. If she'd stayed, they may have been married by now.

If she hadn't gotten pregnant.... Well that was another thing altogether. He wouldn't give up his beautiful baby for anything or anyone.

He contemplated his life without Lily. He felt hollow. As though his heart had been ripped right out of his body.

He couldn't imagine his life without either of them, but he wasn't sure he could forgive Melanie for what she did.

Leaving like that had destroyed him. It had affected his work too. He was so distraught about the loss of someone he'd thought of as his soulmate and couldn't concentrate.

The sheriff had put him on desk duty for a while until he sorted himself out.

It helped, but it didn't heal his broken heart. He'd never really gotten over it.

Out of the blue, Lily began to cry. Jason rubbed her back, but it didn't work. He patted her back, same thing. He took her out into the fresh air, but she continued to cry.

It broke his heart. This tiny little creature had stolen his heart and he never wanted to lose her.

He made a pact with himself there and then.

Somehow, he had to win Melanie back.

He still loved her, despite being angry with her. He had to find a way to move forward and become a normal loving family.

~~~

As much as she loved Lily, Melanie felt as though she was suffocating. She'd been home from hospital for nearly a week and hadn't left the house at all.

Sure, she'd sat outside in the fresh air while the baby slept, even snoozed out there. But she was stuck there at Jason's house. She had no mode of transport of her own and didn't want to ask Jason to take her anywhere.

Besides, he was still mad at her for leaving.
~~~

She thought she was doing the right thing. He'd said several times he was a confirmed bachelor. Looking back though, he'd not said it to her. He'd said it to Aunt Lizzie – who was always trying to marry him off.

She'd even tried to hook him up with Melanie. They'd be going out for some time, so probably thought it was a natural progression.

What had she done? Had she ruined any chance of happiness they might have had?

Melanie stifled a sob as she looked down at her sleeping beauty.

"Melanie," Jason whispered, coming up behind her. "Would you like to go to town? We haven't shopped for you yet." His arms went up around her, but just as quickly dropped down again.

Her heart skipped a beat. Until now, he'd made no effort to get close to her. He'd barely acknowledged her presence some days.

He might as well have been back at work, but the sheriff insisted he have the time off.

She longed to turn back the clock. Wished she'd never left. She should have talked to him – given him the choice.

Her eyes filled with tears and Melanie ran out of the room. She didn't want Jason to see her distress.

This was all her fault.

Totally.

Without a doubt.

She ran into her room and closed the door behind her, then lay on the bed and cried. Not that it would solve her problem, but it would make her feel better.

For now.

"Melanie?" He tapped on the door. "Are you okay?" He tapped again.

"No. Yes," she said quietly, not sure of the answer herself. "I'm getting ready to go out," she said louder. She could lie to herself as much as she liked. It wouldn't change the facts.

She'd ruined her only chance of happiness and may never be able to repair it.

Melanie quickly showered and put on one of her maternity outfits. It was all she had.

She looked at herself in the full-length mirror. She looked horrible. Her hair was a straggly mess, her face was pasty, and her clothes hung off her life a broken mannequin.

She stood with her back against the bedroom door. She didn't want to come out. Didn't want Jason to see her like that.

Had she looked this awful all along? No wonder he wanted to buy new clothes for her. She was a frump.

She couldn't do anything about the maternity clothes which practically fell off her, but she could tie her hair back, and she could put on a bit of makeup.

She gingerly went back to the mirror – she looked better than before. Not perfect, far from it, but better. She braced herself and opened the bedroom door with conviction.

"You look great," Jason said with a smile.

Melanie closed her eyes against the lie. "No I don't," she said as she opened them again. "I look awful. I'm a frump; I feel ugly." She leaned against the wall and look a deep breath.

Her voice was a whisper when she spoke again. "I can't go out looking like this." Her hands waved in the air, indicating what she was wearing. What her hair was like. What she felt like.

Jason stood staring at her. *What did he see?*

He opened his mouth to speak, but instead pulled her into his arms. "You are not a frump," he whispered into her ear. "You are the beautiful soul who gave birth to my daughter."

Her heart skipped a beat. Did he really mean it, or was he just humoring her?

Suddenly he pulled away and she felt bereft. "When is Lily due for a feed," he asked. "We'll leave straight after that."

Melanie checked her watch. "Very soon," she said, and headed to the baby's room. Lily lay in her basinet, her eyes open. Any minute now she'd start crying. Her mother lifted the little bundle and lay her on the change mat, chatting away to the baby as she was changed into a clean diaper.

When she turned around, Jason was standing in the doorway watching her. "What?" she asked, but he just shrugged, a grin on his face.

She pushed her way past, and the contact with his warm body made her think back to a time when they were on better terms.

She continued to the loungeroom and fed Lily.

~~~

Not a word was said on the way into town, although she'd caught Jason stealing glances at her.

He stopped outside the beauty salon, shoved several notes into Melanie's hand and told her to have her hair fixed. "The full treatment," he said.

She looked down into her hand. He'd given her way over a hundred dollars. She sat there shaking her head. "I, I can't," she said. "This is too much."

He watched as the heat rose from her neck, all the way up her face. He was afraid she wasn't going to accept his gift. She'd given him the greatest gift of all, and he wanted to give her something in return.

He climbed out of the driver's seat, took Lily from her carrier and placed her in the buggy, then escorted Melanie into the salon.

A young woman stood at the front counter. "Can I help you?"

Melanie was still shaking her head. "She needs everything," Jason said. "Melanie has just had a baby and says she feels like a frump. She's not; she's gorgeous, she truly is, but she needs to feel that way." He watched as the woman's eyes opened wide, then her mouth formed a huge grin.
~~~

"That's so wonderful," she said. "So, cut, color...?"

"Whatever is needed," he interrupted. "Whatever it takes to make her feel beautiful again."

He watched as the heat crept up Melanie's face again. He wished she didn't feel so poorly about herself.

"Ooooh, I wish you were *my* husband," the beauty salon woman said, as she continued to grin.

But Jason didn't want her. He wanted Melanie. He wanted to win her back. To make her feel whole again.

"How long?" he asked, heading for the door with Lily.

"Two hours. Could be longer," he was told. He nodded and left.

<div align="center">~~~</div>

Melanie surveyed herself in the mirror.

Tears threatened to well in her eyes. She looked beautiful. Truly beautiful.

With her permission, they'd cut her shoulder-length hair to just below her ears and shaped her hair. Rather than an all-over color, they decided on foils. Her brown hair was now tempered with red and blonde streaks, making it look amazing.

They'd given her a neck massage, and also applied light make-up.

She couldn't wait for Jason to come back to see the new Melanie. The one that didn't look like an outcast anymore.

She looked down at her clothes. The smile left her face.

A short time later the door to the salon opened, and Jason entered with Lily in her buggy. His head shot up when he saw her, then he rushed to her side.

"Wow," he said. "That's an amazing transformation." He smiled at the beauty therapist. "You did a wonderful job. Thank you so much."

Then he looked at Melanie. He leaned in and whispered in her ear. "You were beautiful already, but now you look like a movie star." He kissed her cheek and stood again.

Her heart leapt. Did he really think that, or was he just saying it to make her feel better?

After they'd paid, they left the salon quickly. "The dress shop is just around the corner. We can go there next if you like," Jason told her.

Melanie laughed. "Do you mean the boutique?" She liked when she laughed. It made her feel good, and she sure didn't feel that way much lately.

"And yes please. I need to dump these horrid rags."

His smile faded. She was a kill-joy. She knew it and he knew it. She was trying, she truly was, but she was only saying what she knew to be true.

They entered the boutique and she was in her element. They had the most beautiful clothes, which surprised her since it was a small-town boutique. She didn't think the range would be so intensive.

The sales assistant helped her to choose a number of clothes and guided her to the changing rooms. Jason sat patiently, rocking the buggy while she tried on clothes.

She came out to show him an outfit she liked, and he watched intently. "You look great," he said, smiling. She liked the outfit and put it aside.

She showed him each outfit, and he nodded each time, smiling at the same time. At the end, she didn't know which ones to take.

He intervened. "We'll take them all," Jason told the assistant.

Melanie was horrified. "No! It's too much," she protested, but he would have none of it.

They walked out of the store with several bags of clothes, including the outfit Melanie had arrived in.

She moved close to him. "Thank you, Jason," she said, her arm rubbing against his. "I am truly grateful. I don't know how I'll ever repay you."

He stared at her, frowning. "This is a gift, Melanie," he said crossly. "I don't expect you to repay me."

"I must," she said quietly. "I mean..."

He interrupted her mid-sentence. "You're the mother of my baby. I *will* look after you both."

She was stunned. *Was that all she was to him? The mother of his baby?* Her heart sank. She felt hollow. Truly saddened.

Melanie wanted to cry, but she was not going to let him see how upset she was.

They walked silently back to his vehicle, depositing their purchases, then walked further up the road to Aunt Lizzie's Kitchen.

"We'll have lunch here," Jason said. "I don't know about you, but I'm famished."

Melanie nodded, but her appetite had suddenly disappeared.

The little bell on the door tinkled as they entered.

Aunt Lizzie came running when she saw the buggy. "Oooooh, she's beautiful," she said, staring down at the sleeping baby. "How are you feeling, Melanie," she asked. "You look wonderful. Not doing too much, I hope?"

Jason pulled her closer and put his arm up around her shoulders. It felt wonderful but was all for show. But she put her hand on his and savored the moment.

Her heart was beating rapidly at the contact, but she knew it would be over way too soon.

"She does look wonderful," he said, looking down into Melanie's face. "She's beautiful." He smiled at her, and Melanie's heart swelled, but she knew it was just pretend.

"Ah, young love," Lizzie said, smiling at them both. "So what is it? Coffee or lunch?"

Melanie wasn't sure how long she could keep up the pretense.

"Lunch. Definitely lunch," Jason said. "I'm starving."

They were reading over the menu when Lizzie returned. "So when do you go back to work, Jason? You seemed to have been on leave for ages."

Melanie cringed. Lizzie was right. It had been a little over two weeks already. Surely he'd have to go back soon? They hadn't even discussed it. Or what would happen when he did go back.

Did he expect her and Lily to leave then? Or was he going to let them stay on a little longer? She sure hoped so.

She had no idea where they would go. With no family, they had nowhere to go.

Jason covered her hand with his. "I'm not going back for at least another couple of weeks," he said looking across to Melanie. "I have a ton of leave owing, and the sheriff insisted I take at least a month off."

He squeezed her hand and smiled. "Melanie might be sick of me by then."

Lizzie stared at him. "A handsome and generous young fella such as yourself? Never," she said.

Melanie echoed Lizzie's thoughts. She would never get sick of Jason. She loved him. With all her heart. She just wished he would love her back.

Chapter Four

Lizzie offered to look after Lily, so they could have a night out.

Melanie was both excited and apprehensive. Jason could understand that; he felt the same way.

This would be the first time they'd left her alone with anyone.

It was normal to feel this way, he knew it was. Other new parents had told him, Rory and Missy included.

They'd done it and they'd survived. Baby Chloe had lived through it, and they would too.

Lily would probably sleep through the whole thing anyway.

They would have dinner at a restaurant in nearby Boulton, then go to a movie. There wasn't a lot of choice, but Melanie had chosen a popular romantic comedy. Not his cup of tea, but for Melanie, he'd sit through it.

He'd booked a table at the prestigious new restaurant that had opened a few months earlier. It had a reputation for having amazing food.

They stood inside the door waiting to be seated, when the Maître d' approached them.

"Sir, Madam," he said, and led them to their table.

Jason watched as Melanie's face lit up at being treated as special. As she sat, he whipped out the napkin and placed it in her lap.

He then turned her glass and filled it with water. He studied her face. It was obvious to Jason she felt like a movie star.

He really needed to take her out more often.

Then they were left alone, and Jason stared into her eyes. They were beautiful. The windows to her soul. Only she wasn't letting him in. He desperately wanted in.

He wasn't sure what he needed to do to get through to her, but he was sure going to try. His heart broke every time she turned away from him. Every time she rejected his advances.

He loved her with all his heart. Would do anything for her.

Hell, he would die for her.

"Melanie," he whispered. "This is a pretty posh place."

She laughed and her whole face lit up. "It sure is," she whispered back.

He reached across the table and grabbed her hand. She looked at their entwined hands, but her face was giving nothing away.

He gave it a gentle squeeze. "I," He was interrupted by their waiter.

"Your menus," he said, handing them each a menu to peruse.

Jason felt cross, although he knew he shouldn't. This was a restaurant – the waiters were doing normal restaurant things, like look after their customers.

But he wanted time alone with Melanie, and it wasn't happening. He sighed. At least at the cinema they would be alone.

The food here was amazing. Better than he'd ever imagined, and knew they'd return. That was, if he could get Melanie to stay on.

His breath hitched, and his heart did a hiccup. Would he be successful? He sure hoped so. He didn't want to lose either of them.

He looked down into his food. What would it take to get Melanie to trust him again?

He lifted his head to find Melanie staring at him. "What are you thinking?"

She was studying his face, and he felt suddenly subconscious. "Nothing much," he said, pushing his food around the plate. "How amazing this food is. How we should come back. How much I missed you when you were gone."

Did he really say that?

"I missed you too, Jason." She said it so quietly he almost missed it.

He reached across and covered her hand, rubbing his thumb across it absently. He was about to respond, opened his mouth to speak, when the waiter interrupted them. Again.

"Your dessert menu," he said handing a list over to each of them. "I recommend for you..."

Jason turned off, and instead, stared into Melanie's eyes.

They were beautiful, her eyes. Just like the woman herself. He reached out and his fingers caressed her cheek. Her expression softened, and her face molded to his hand.

"Melanie, I,"

"Your dessert, Sir, Madam. I shall return with your coffee shortly."

Jason sighed. The service here was admirable, but it was too much. Perfect for most people, but he wanted more privacy. Time to talk to Melanie. To tell her how he felt.

She looked down at her dessert. "This looks incredible," she said, and smiled at him. "Thank you for bringing me here."

But her smile quickly faded. "Melanie? What's wrong," he asked, covering her hand once more.

"I forgot about Lily," she said. "I'm enjoying myself so much I forgot about our baby. I'm a horrible mother."

Jason laughed, and she glared at him. He sighed and pulled out his cell phone. "Lizzie? Melanie wants to check on Lily." He glanced across to Melanie and nodded. "Sure. Thank you," he said. "And Lizzie? We both appreciate it. A lot."

He finished the call, then directed his words to Melanie.

"She's perfectly fine and has only woken once. Lizzie changed her diaper and she went back to sleep shortly afterwards."

He squeezed her hand. "It's completely normal to worry," he said. "Especially since this is the first time leaving our precious little girl."

Melanie nodded, but still seemed unhappy. "Eat your dessert. The movie will be starting soon."

He didn't like her being unhappy. She deserved to be happy. Deliriously happy. He needed to fix that. Would fix that – sooner rather than later.

~~~

Melanie snuggled up as close to Jason as she could get, but it wasn't close enough.

Cinema seats are not conducive to lovers or would-be lovers. They were geared more toward people wanting to watch a movie.

They sat at the back, where it was near empty. Jason had been pedantic about sitting where they'd have more privacy. And Melanie was more than a little happy about that.
~~~

So far, all they'd seen were advertisements. The main feature, the movie, was what they'd come for. She had carefully chosen a romantic movie, hoping Jason might get the hint.

He was the nicest man she knew, more than generous, and he treated her like a princess.

More than a princess, he made her feel like a queen. But what was the point of that if he didn't return her love?

Melanie died a little more inside every time she thought about it.

The advertisements ended, the curtains closed, and the lights went down, bringing her out of her thoughts. Then just as quickly the curtains opened again, and the movie began.

It was the age-old story. Man and woman meet, they fall in love, but there are obstacles to their love.

Much the same as their situation. She bit back a sob as her eyes filled with tears.

As though he knew, Jason reached across and held her hand. He offered her popcorn, but Melanie waved him away. She didn't dare speak for fear of breaking down.

Right there, and right now.

She felt the warmth of his big hand and felt somewhat comforted. "Jason," she whispered, against her better judgement. He leaned into her.

As he turned, she shook her head, changing her mind. *Coward!*

What was she meant to say? *I love you dearly, can you please love me back? Even if it's only for the sake of our daughter?*

No. That would never work, and she wouldn't want it to. She wanted all or nothing, and the way things were going, it would be nothing.

She felt errant tears trickle down her face.

Jason didn't love her. Not in the true sense.

Sure, he had feelings for her. They would never have had a baby together otherwise. But he'd never come out and told her he loved her. Never said those three magic words.

The words every woman longs to hear from the man she believes to be her soulmate.

Communication was never their strong point. Jason's work consumed him a lot of the time. It wasn't like a 9-5 job where you could turn it on and off. As much as Melanie would have liked it to be.

Even when they were out on a date, if someone broke the law, Jason would step in.

Melanie groaned quietly. It was one of the things she loved about him, and yet, it was also one of the things that had threatened to tear them apart.

Maybe that was why the sheriff had insisted he have so much time off? To force them get to know each other all over again without interruption.

Clever man, that sheriff.

He leaned into her. "Good movie," he whispered, then kissed her lightly on the cheek.

Suddenly his hand went up to her face. "What's wrong?" he asked urgently.

She swiped at her cheeks, trying to hide the tears. "Nothing's wrong," she said quietly, lying to not only herself, but also to Jason.

"Tell me," he said, worry in his voice.

She waved her hands in the air and forced herself to breath. This was neither the time or the place. "Hormones," she whispered. "Nothing to worry about."

She watched as he let go of the breath he'd been holding, then he squeezed her hand again.

She liked it when he touched her. *No. She loved it when he touched her.* It didn't have to be an intimate type of touch. Just holding her close or holding her hand like he was now.

It made her feel good all over. She really missed the way they used to be. Before she left. Before she ruined both their lives by not telling him they were having a baby.

She turned back to the movie, but Melanie could feel his eyes on her. Watching her, studying her every move. It took all her effort not to turn her head and look at him.

"Melanie," he said quietly.

She slowly turned toward him, and his hands came up, cupping her face. He began to lean into her.

Melanie looked into his eyes. His eyes that always got to her. They were beautiful, and they were unique. Sometimes she felt like she could see right down to his core when she stared into them.

She studied his face. He had laughter lines around his eyes as well as his mouth. Jason was so special to her, and she wanted to know every little bit of him.

His tongue darted out of his mouth, and he licked his lips. Her hand went up and touched his whiskers. She loved the way he always left a shadow on his chin when he shaved. It was very appealing. Sexy even.

She watched as he continued to move slowly toward her, and her heart rate went up. She felt it in her chest, in her throat, and in her head.

Why was she reacting like this?

Jason closed the distance between them and gently kissed her lips. Melanie felt light-headed with excitement.

Was this the first step toward mending their relationship? She certainly hoped so.

~~~

Jason's heart raced, and he felt sweat forming on his forehead.

The closer he got, the faster his heart seemed to beat. This was crazy. He'd kissed Melanie before. Loads of times.

Of course, that was before.

Before she'd abandoned him without a word.
~~~

Without telling him she was pregnant with his baby.

Giving him no choice.

For a heart-beat he considered backing off. His eyes locked with hers and he saw them pleading with him.

He wasn't going to change his mind. He wanted to kiss her.

And he certainly wasn't averse to kissing her soft lips.

As he moved in, she closed her eyes gently, and let herself lean into him. She tasted of popcorn and pop, and he savored the moment.

He heard her softly moan, and he smiled against her lips.

The kiss only lasted seconds, but it felt like forever.

It seemed like a lifetime since he'd kissed her. Since he'd held her tight. And since they'd been as one.

When the kiss ended, he embraced her. One arm came up around her, the other still holding the popcorn, damn it.

Without a second thought, Jason dumped the container of popcorn on the floor and held her tight. He felt Melanie's arms go around him, and the rest of the world disappeared.

Nothing mattered except Melanie, right here in his arms. His beautiful Melanie, the one he thought he'd lost all those months ago.

"Tell me I haven't lost you," he whispered in her ear, his voice raspy with emotion.

Her lack of response was breaking his heart. "Melanie?" He pushed back and looked into her face.

She licked her lips before speaking. "It's going to be... difficult," she said softly, the movie still playing in the background. "I've lost your trust." Her voice was breaking, but she continued. "And that's on me."

She leaned forward and back into his embrace. "I want this to work out, I really do," she whispered in his ear. "If for no other reason, but for Lily."

Before tonight, Jason had no idea what it would feel like when your heart shattered.

CHAPTER FIVE

Jason stood looking down into Lily's basinet.

He did not want to leave his baby. Didn't want to do this at all; it was heartbreaking. But he had to return to work.

He'd had his month of leave, and now had to go back to being a police officer and not only a dad.

He swallowed hard.

How did other fathers do this?

He'd thoroughly enjoyed the time he'd had at home. Loved the long walks with Lily in her buggy, the times cuddling her when she cried, and had especially enjoyed her bath-times.

He always felt at home in his uniform, but today he just wanted to rip it off. It felt almost suffocating, but he was fully aware it was more about leaving Lily than anything.

He continued to stare at the baby as she slept and didn't hear Melanie come up behind him. "Ready to go," she whispered, putting her arms up around his waist.

Jason nodded not trusting himself to speak. He felt so emotional right now, he was sure his voice would break. And that would not do.

Melanie turned to him and straightened his collar, letting her hands linger on his arms. He straightened his back against the feelings her touch evoked.

They looked into each other's eyes for what seemed an eternity.

He leaned forward and moved toward Melanie's lips. He so wanted to kiss her like this. Instead he changed direction and kissed her on the forehead instead.

He heard her softly sigh.

He'd hurt her feelings. He knew he had, but there wasn't a lot he could do about it right now. He had to go. He leaned down and lightly kissed Lily on the cheek.

"I don't know what time I'll be home," he said, heading for the door.

Melanie lifted her hand to his cheek, where she let it linger. "Stay safe," she said softly, as though she really meant it.

If only she did mean it. If only she truly cared.

Right now he was nothing but a meal ticket. Someone to look after her. How he wished that would change.

He wanted Melanie to love him. To truly love him the way he loved her.

He sat in his vehicle and slammed his fist on the steering wheel. He was a bloody fool. *He* was the one who never said the words. Who never told her how he felt.

And the one who never made the commitment like he'd intended.

That needed to change. Melanie had always been a woman of few words, and he totally understood why. Until they'd met, she'd been a drifter.

He'd found her on the side of the road one day, huddled in newspaper, waiting for the bus to arrive. With no family, and no friends, she had nowhere to stay.

He'd set her up in a local hostel and taken her under his wing. It hadn't taken long before he'd realized he had feelings for her.

Naturally he'd fought those feelings. He was doing his job, looking after her. He'd found her during a routine check while he was out on patrol.

But he'd taken it further. He'd made sure she was okay. That she had somewhere to stay. Organized assistance for her, but he'd crossed the line.

He'd taken her to dinner, and even a movie or two. He'd told himself he was just looking out for her.

For months he'd denied how he felt. Until one day the feelings were so strong, he could no longer lie to himself.

They'd been dating for nearly a year when she suddenly disappeared. His heart was torn into a million pieces, but Jason put it down to her drifter tendencies.

Never in a million years did he think she would be pregnant with his baby. His beautiful Lily.

His throat closed over.

He had two choices. He could continue the way they were, and skirt around each other at home. Spend his time with Lily and only communicating with Melanie when he needed to, which was breaking his heart.

Or he could tell Melanie how he truly felt, and they could go back to being a couple. A real couple.

Sure, everyone in River Valley thought they were a couple, and they hadn't said otherwise. But he wanted to put things right between them. He was in love with Melanie. Head over heels totally in love.

He wanted to marry her.

He took a deep breath.

Before she left, he'd already decided to propose. To finally tell her how much he loved her.

But she didn't give him the opportunity. He woke up and she was gone.

Without a word.

Without so much as a note.

Nothing.

Nada.

Zilch.

His heart had shattered.

Sure he'd tried to find her, to find out what happened to her, but she was good at disappearing. She'd done it most of her life.

Jason sat in the carpark of the Sheriff's Office, thinking about how he would ask her, when there was a knock on the side window.

"Jason, come on," Sheriff Chase Callahan said. "We have a call. I need you now!"

He jumped out of the vehicle and ran inside for his weapon. He was back in just a few minutes.

"You drive, I'll coordinate," the sheriff said.

It was good to be back.

~~~

Lights and sirens flashed, and cars were everywhere. The police, fire department, and even ambulances were nearby.

A bank robbery gone wrong, which had turned into a hostage situation.

Jason's heart was pounding. Adrenalin was pouring through his veins. It was good to be back, but all he could do was think of Melanie and Lily.

What if something happened and he never got to tell Melanie how he felt? Never got to see his little girl grow up?
~~~

They sat outside the bank for a little over two hours with no movement from inside. The negotiator worked hard to get the perpetrators to give themselves up. When they thought it would never happen, finally the door to the bank opened.

"Hands in the air!" The negotiator stepped forward, and the two masked men complied.

They all breathed a sigh of relief.

They were handcuffed without incidence and placed in a police vehicle.

"I wish they were all that easy," Jason said, heading back to his police vehicle.

"Totally," Chase replied.

They returned to the Sheriff's Office in silence, both mentally exhausted from the morning's encounter.

"Jason." Chase indicated for him to follow the sheriff to his office. "Shut the door and sit down."

Jason swallowed hard. He had no idea what this was about.

Chase leaned back in his chair and put his hands behind his head casually. "How are things at home?"

His relief was palpable, and Jason sighed. "Good," he said without conviction. "We're getting there."

Chase silently stared at him, then put his arms down on the desk. He leaned forward and spoke quietly. "You need to sort this out, Jason." He leaned back in his chair.

Jason nodded, but said nothing.

"It's going to eat you up and tear you both apart. And..." He took a deep breath before continuing. "I know you don't want to hear this, but that little girl needs both her parents."

Jason opened his mouth to speak but Chase held up a finger to stop him.

"She deserves to have parents who love each other."

"I know," Jason said, looking down into his lap. "But I'm not sure how to make that happen."

The sheriff stood and stared out the window, his back to Jason. "It's none of my business, we both know that. But I've known you a long time and want you to be happy." He turned to face Jason again.

"You're one of my best officers. I don't want to lose you because you're too stubborn to tell Melanie you love her."

Chase laughed a bitter laugh. "I've been down that track myself. It's not worth it. Stop denying your feelings."

Jason sat stunned and didn't utter a word. Didn't move, didn't bat an eyelid.

"Yeah, yeah," Chase said, waving his arms about. "None of my business, I know. But I need my staff to be happy and stable."

The sheriff looked down as his pager went off. "Right," he said. "Work to do."

Jason nodded then left.

His brain was clicking over at a million miles an hour.

He left the Sheriff's Office that night with a plan, and a huge weight off his shoulders.

~~~

Lizzie arrived right on time.

Lily had been fed and bathed, and Melanie was getting ready to put her down for the night. She was taken aback when she saw Lizzie sitting in their loungeroom. "Lizzie," she said. "This is a surprise." She frowned, and Lizzie smiled. Jason purposely hadn't told Melanie about his plans.

She had the baby in her arms and had brought her for Jason to say goodnight. He leaned in and kissed his precious girl on the forehead. "Goodnight, my darling," he said softly.

"She's such a dear," Lizzie said.

"Would you like a cuddle before she goes to bed," Melanie asked Lizzie, still clearly puzzled.

"Of course," the older woman said. "I'll take care of her while you get ready if you want." Lizzie winked at Jason, while Melanie looked totally confused.

He closed the few steps between them and pulled Melanie to him. "It's a surprise," he whispered in her ear. "Lizzie offered to look after Lily, so we can go out."
~~~

She pulled back to look at him, a huge smile on her face. "Really? Oh Lizzie, that's so wonderful," she said. "Thank you from the bottom of my heart."

"I almost forgot," Jason said. "Wait here." He indicated for Melanie to wait, then left the room, coming back a short time later.

The look on her face was priceless. "These are for you," he said, handing over a huge bunch of red roses. *Red for love,* Lizzie had told him.

He watched as Melanie blinked back tears, and her bottom lip quivered. "Thank you," she almost whispered. "They're beautiful." She stepped forward and gave him a big hug.

Lizzie gave him the thumbs up. "Don't worry about Lily," she said. "You get yourself organised for your big date. I'll sort this one out." Melanie kissed the baby lightly on the cheek, then held Lizzie's hand.

"You are so wonderful, Lizzie," she said, conviction in her voice. "I don't know what we'd do without you."

As she left the room, Melanie turned again and mouthed *thank you* to Lizzie.

Jason could see her excitement bubbling up, barely controlled. "Thank you from me too, Lizzie," he said. "You have no idea what this means to me."

"I think I do," she said, holding the baby close. "You and Melanie deserve all the happiness you can get." She reached out with her free hand and took his, holding it tight. "You know what to do," she said. "It could be your last chance."

He nodded. "I know," he said quietly. "I just hope I don't blow it."

Lizzie's face softened. "You won't," she said. "Just tell her how you feel. Melanie will appreciate that. At least this way you'll know where you stand."

She squeezed his hand. "Go and spruce yourself up. It's nearly time to leave."

He nodded then left the room. So far, everything was going to plan.

~~~

"Where are we going?" Until now, Melanie had sat quietly in the passenger seat. "This doesn't look like the way to a restaurant." He smiled. Of course she would assume that.

"Not a restaurant. We are going to dinner, but first I wanted to take you up into the Montana Hills. To the lookout. I've never taken you there before."

He glanced across at her. She didn't sound convinced. "It's a very special place," he said softly, and she nodded. "We're nearly there."

About ten minutes later they pulled into the lookout carpark.

"It's really dark," she said, climbing out. "Scary even."

He darted around to her side of the vehicle. "Don't stress," he said, taking her hand. "I won't leave your side, I promise."

They walked quietly to the lookout, and Jason pushed his hand into hers. Melanie let him.
~~~

"Here we are," he said. "Isn't it beautiful?"

Melanie looked around, taking in the skyline, the homes that were littered about, and the tiny township.

"It is," she said. "Stunning. Totally gorgeous." She took a deep breath. "I had no idea this lookout was up here." She turned to him and gently punched his arm. "Why haven't you brought me here before?" She was genuinely curious.

"I don't know," he said, knowing it was a total lie. He'd intended bringing her here to propose, but she'd absconded before he could.

He swallowed hard and licked his lips. The memory shattered his composure, and he was on the verge of stomping on his plans for the evening. Bringing everything forward.

But he had to stick to the plan.

Melanie moved closer, and he pulled her to him, deciding to forge ahead. She looked up into his face and smiled. "It's not so scary anymore," she whispered. "I feel safe with you."

He looked down into her eyes in the darkness. They glittered from the moonlight, and he swore he could see her soul. "Melanie," he whispered, as though there were eavesdroppers around them.

The expression on her face was pure innocence mixed with... What?

He wasn't sure. But he hoped what he was seeing was at the very least, adoration. What he really wanted to see was love. He wasn't sure whether he was or not.

As he continued to stare, she licked her lips. Her arms went up around his neck, and she pulled him to her. "Jason," she whispered. "Shut up and kiss me."

He closed the distance between them, and gently kissed her lips. Her eyes were closed, and she was totally relaxed. Her body fell against his, and he reveled in her nearness.

He brushed his lips softly along hers and waited for her reaction. He felt her pull him closer still. Suddenly her lips covered his. Her arms moved down his back, and he liked the way it felt.

"Melanie," he whispered reluctantly. "I have a table booked. We have to go."

Her saw the silhouette of her nodding in the darkness, then she pulled her hands away. He felt bereft without the warmth of her touch. He took both her hands in his. "I'm sorry," he said, and meant it.

It was all well and good to have a plan, but sometimes the best laid plans went awry. Tonight though, everything needed to go like clockwork.

She studied his face in the darkness. "Don't be sorry," she said, the moon dancing in her eyes. "This place is beautiful. I'm really glad you brought me here."

He opened the door for her and felt as though he was beginning to break down the barrier between them. "We'll come back another time," he promised, before making his way to the driver's side.

"Jason," she said, placing her hand on his knee as he drove. "Thanks for tonight. It was a lovely surprise."

Warmth spread from his knee to his entire body. He couldn't stop the grin that began to form. "You are very welcome," he said, chancing a quick glance her way before turning back to the road.

It wasn't long before they pulled up out the front of Aunt Lizzie's Kitchen.

Melanie looked confused. "Ah, you do know they're not open tonight?" She glanced at him, a frown forming. "I mean, Lizzie is at our place. How..."

He chuckled. "Just wait and see."

She still looked confused as he helped her out and led her toward the entrance. The blinds were all pulled down, but they could see soft light coming from beneath them.

Jason knocked, and Charlotte Dolan answered the door. She waved them in and locked the door behind them.

"You know Charlotte, don't you, Melanie?" When she shook her head, Jason introduced them. "Charlotte is married to Officer Chris Dolan. You know Chris, right?" He didn't wait for an answer. "This is Melanie Bishop," he told Charlotte, and the two women shook hands.

Lizzie had promised it would be spectacular and it was.

The light was muted, and she'd pulled most of the tables back against the wall until there was only one table in the center of the room.

The table was decorated formally and had two candles burning in the middle of it. It was very romantic with the shadow of the candlelight flickering on the walls.

Charlotte led them to their table and seated them both. She winked at Jason, then left them alone, heading for the kitchen.

Soft music played in the background, and Jason reached over and covered Melanie's hand with his own. A thrill went through his hand and ran all the way up his arm. Warmth spread through him.

He loved the feeling he got when he touched Melanie, and when he was with her. She was his soulmate. He was more sure of that than anything else in his life.

"You continue to surprise me," Melanie said. "I didn't think you had a romantic bone in your body."

He wasn't sure if he should be offended or happy. With help from dear Lizzie, he'd gone all out for Melanie tonight and certainly hoped it came across as romantic.

Charlotte came out a short time later with their entrée; cheese and salmon puffs.

"Tuck in," she said, then disappeared again, returning almost immediately with a decanter of iced water, which she poured into glasses.

"This is amazing," Melanie told Charlotte, who smiled at the compliment.

Jason sang Charlotte's praises. "She's a fully qualified chef," he told her. "Charlotte runs the business with Lizzie now."

Charlotte quickly disappeared and left them to their own devices.

They finished their entrées and Melanie wiped her mouth with a napkin. "I wonder if Lily is asleep," she said quietly.

Jason flashed her a smile. "Lizzie will call if there's a problem," he said, not wanting anything to distract them from *their* special night. Besides, he knew Lizzie would only call if it was an emergency.

Charlotte arrived with the next course, coq au vin. It was beautifully presented, with the chicken dish placed on a bed of mash, and fresh beans on the side.

She'd already placed a basket of freshly baked bread rolls in the center of the table.

Jason's mouth was watering, but he couldn't lose focus of the evening's purpose.

"Oh my." Melanie was impressed. He knew it from the moment they entered the little café. He'd do anything to make her happy, and he prayed she was beginning to understand that.

"How did you organise this," she asked, waving her hands about. "It's amazing. Thank you," she said, and Jason's heart felt happy.

"Anything for you," he said, and she smiled coyly before taking a mouthful of food.

"Mmmmmmm. This is… I have no words to describe it," she continued.

Jason grinned at her. "I know, right?" He'd been fortunate enough to have sampled Charlotte's food on several occasions.

When they finished eating, Charlotte cleared their dishes away and retreated to the kitchen again, leaving them to talk.

He wasn't sure where to start. "Melanie," he said, reaching across the table to hold her hand. "You know I have feelings for you." That didn't come out the way he meant. What he really wanted to say was *I love you with all my heart.* Why wouldn't his brain coordinate with his heart?

He sighed. This wasn't going so well. And he'd only just started.

She started to pull her hand away. "I mean…" He had to find a way to resurrect this conversation.

He stretched his neck and shoulders. He was starting to feel stressed.

Jason stood and went to the DVD player, turning up the soft music a notch or two, then presenting himself to Melanie.

"May I have this dance, Mademoiselle?" He bowed in front of her and took her hand, leading her to the tiny area Lizzie had strategically arranged for that purpose.

"You know I can't dance," Melanie told him, giggling. It was nice to hear her happy. He loved the tinkling sound she made when she giggled.

His mouth moved into a slow smile. "Neither can I," he said. "But who cares?"

When they arrived at their designated spot, Jason pulled her gently to him, holding one hand, and wrapping one arm around her.

It felt nice to hold her again. Even if she was stiff as a board.

He let go her hand and caressed her cheek. "Relax," he said, and she loosened up a little.

They shuffled around the room, and he felt her go loose, until finally she let her whole body relax against his. Her head tucked into his chest, just under his chin, and he finally felt ready.

Ready to put the rest of his life in her hands.

"This is nice," she said softly, her arms going up around his back, pulling him closer.

His hand came up and tucked a strand of hair behind her ear. "Melanie," he said quietly, knowing he sounded nervous. "I need to tell you something." By now his voice was breaking up. This was harder than he'd ever imagined.

She looked up at him. "Is everything alright?" Then she stopped dead. "You're kicking us out, aren't you?" Tears welled in her eyes.

"What? No." This was not what he'd planned. *Why would she even think that?*

Tears trickled down her face, and he wiped them away with his thumb. "I've been so stupid," she said, the tears continuing to flow. "Why didn't I tell you before how much I love you? Now it's too late."

Jason froze. She loved him? *She loved him?*

What a fool he'd been. "Oh my gosh, Melanie. I brought you here tonight to tell you how much I love you."

She stared at him in disbelief. "No you didn't. You're just saying that because I said it first."

This was definitely not going to plan. He'd not even considered this scenario. Now he wasn't sure what to do next. So he went with his gut. "You're wrong," he said quietly, and reached into his pocket, pulling out a tiny box. "I brought you here tonight to ask you to marry me."

He opened the box and pulling out the precious piece, placed it on her finger. Then he dropped to one knee and held her hand. "Melanie, will you marry me?"

She stood staring down at him. Her gaze went from his eyes to the ring and back again. Time slowed down. She was going to turn him down, he was certain.

"Yes!" she finally said and wrapped her arms around his neck.

Jason stood and pulled her close. "I love you so much," he said, then his lips covered hers, and they were lost in each other.

~~~

The little chapel sat on a hill not far outside the township of River Valley. It had been getting a good workout over the past few months.
~~~

Jason and Melanie stood out the front, holding their precious baby girl as the preacher asked each of them to repeat their wedding vows.

He still couldn't believe Melanie had said yes. He was standing with the two most important people in his life, and it felt like a dream.

He glanced over his shoulder and saw Chris and Charlotte, and of course Lizzie, along with Rory, Missy and baby Chloe, as well as the rest of the Callahan clan. Some colleagues from the Sheriff's Office were there, Josh Wrangler, Lucas Drury, and Nate Holden, to mention just a few.

They didn't want a big wedding but preferred something more cozy. This was a day to remember, and he only wanted his most favorite people to be there.

When the intimate ceremony was over, he turned to his beautiful bride. "I love you with all my heart, and will cherish you forever," he said.

"I love you too," Melanie said, then kissed him gently on the lips. They pulled Lily into a group hug, and all was right with his world.

THE END

Multi-published, best selling and award-winning author, Cheryl Wright, former secretary, debt collector, account manager, writing coach, and shopping tour hostess, loves reading.

She writes both contemporary and historical western romance, as well as contemporary romance and romantic suspense.

She lives in Melbourne, Australia, and is married with two adult children and has six grandchildren.

When she's not writing, she can be found in her craft room making greeting cards.

Check out Cheryl's Amazon page - *https://www.amazon.com/Cheryl-Wright/e/B0088GDSKM* for a full list of her other books.